Dear Parents:

Congratulations! Your child is taking the first steps on an exciting journey. The destination? Independent reading!

D1072278

STEP INTO READING® will help your child get there. The program offers five steps to reading success. Each step includes fun stories and colorful art or photographs. In addition to original fiction and books with favorite characters, there are Step into Reading Non-Fiction Readers, Phonics Readers and Boxed Sets, Sticker Readers, and Comic Readers—a complete literacy program with something to interest every child.

Learning to Read, Step by Step!

Ready to Read   Preschool–Kindergarten
• big type and easy words • rhyme and rhythm • picture clues
For children who know the alphabet and are eager to begin reading.

Reading with Help   Preschool–Grade 1
• basic vocabulary • short sentences • simple stories
For children who recognize familiar words and sound out new words with help.

Reading on Your Own   Grades 1–3
• engaging characters • easy-to-follow plots • popular topics
For children who are ready to read on their own.

Reading Paragraphs   Grades 2–3
• challenging vocabulary • short paragraphs • exciting stories
For newly independent readers who read simple sentences with confidence.

Ready for Chapters   Grades 2–4
• chapters • longer paragraphs • full-color art
For children who want to take the plunge into chapter books but still like colorful pictures.

STEP INTO READING® is designed to give every child a successful reading experience. The grade levels are only guides; children will progress through the steps at their own speed, developing confidence in their reading. The F&P Text Level on the back cover serves as another tool to help you choose the right book for your child.

Remember, a lifetime love of reading starts with a single step!

To Jill Parker
and Nancy McKay,
who helped me learn
how to read

Copyright © 2014 by Tad Hills
All rights reserved. Published in the United States by Schwartz & Wade Books, an imprint of
Random House Children's Books, a division of Random House LLC, a Penguin Random House
Company, New York.
Step into Reading, Schwartz & Wade Books, and the Schwartz & Wade colophon are registered
trademarks of Random House LLC.
Visit us on the Web!
StepIntoReading.com
randomhouse.com/kids
Educators and librarians, for a variety of teaching tools, visit us at
RHTeachersLibrarians.com
Library of Congress Cataloging-in-Publication Data
Hills, Tad.
Drop it, Rocket / Tad Hills.
pages cm
Summary: "Rocket loves to collect words for his word tree with his teacher, the little
yellow bird. Watch as the pup finds new words like leaf, hat, star, boot, and many more"
—Provided by publisher.
ISBN 978-0-385-37247-3 (hardback) — ISBN 978-0-385-37248-0 (glb)
ISBN 978-0-385-37249-7 (ebook) — ISBN 978-0-385-37254-1 (pbk.)
[1. Vocabulary—Fiction. 2. Dogs—Fiction. 3. Birds—Fiction.] I. Title.
PZ7.H563737Dr 2014
[E]—dc23
2013041866
The illustrations in this book were rendered in colored pencils and acrylic paint.
Printed in the United States of America
22 21 20 19
This book has been officially leveled by using the F & P Text Level Gradient™ Leveling System.

Drop It, Rocket!

by Tad Hills

Random House 🏠 New York

Rocket and
the little yellow bird
love words.

They love
their word tree,
too.

"Are you ready
to find new words
for our word tree?"
asks the bird.

"Yes, I am!"
says Rocket.

Rocket finds a leaf.

"Drop it, Rocket,"
says the bird.

Rocket drops the leaf.

He is a good dog.

Rocket finds a hat.

"Drop it, Rocket."

Rocket drops the hat.

"Good boy."

Rocket finds a star.

"Drop it, Rocket."

Rocket drops the star.

"Good boy."

Rocket finds a red boot.

"Drop it, Rocket,"
says the bird.

"Drop it, Rocket."

"Drop it, Rocket."

Rocket likes the boot.

He will not drop it.

"Will you drop it
for a ball?"
asks the bird.

Rocket will not drop it.

"Will you drop it
for a stick?"
asks Emma.

Rocket will not drop it.

"Will you drop it
for a sock?"
asks Fred.

Rocket will not drop it.

"I have an idea!"
says Owl.

Owl finds a book.

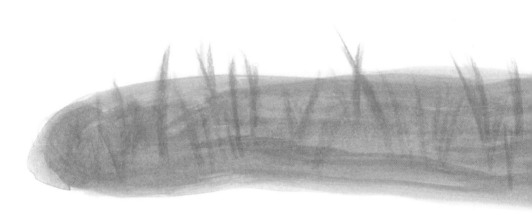

"Will you drop it
for a book?"
asks Owl.

Rocket drops the boot.

"Rocket dropped it!"
says the bird.

Rocket is a good dog.